PUFFIN BOOKS

Bug Brother

Pete Johnson has been a film extra, a film critic for Radio One, an English teacher and a journalist. However, his dream was always to be a writer. At the age of ten he wrote a fan letter to Dodie Smith, author of *The Hundred and One Dalmatians*, and they wrote to each other for many years. Dodie Smith was the first person to encourage him to be a writer.

He has written many books for children as well as plays for the theatre and Radio Four, and is a popular visitor to schools and libraries.

Some other books by Pete Johnson

MIND READER
MIND READER: BLACKMAIL

PETE JOHNSON

BUG BROTHER

Illustrated by Mike Gordon

PUFFIN BOOKS

PUFFIN BOOKS

Published by the Penguin Group
Penguin Books Ltd, 80 Strand, London WC2R 0RL, England
Penguin Putnam Inc., 375 Hudson Street, New York, New York 10014, USA
Penguin Books Australia Ltd, 250 Camberwell Road, Camberwell, Victoria 3124, Australia
Penguin Books Canada Ltd, 10 Alcorn Avenue, Toronto, Ontario, Canada M4V 3B2
Penguin Books India (P) Ltd, 11 Community Centre, Panchsheel Park, New Delhi – 110 017, India
Penguin Books (NZ) Ltd, Cnr Rosedale and Airborne Roads, Albany, Auckland, New Zealand
Penguin Books (South Africa) (Pty) Ltd, 24 Sturdee Avenue, Rosebank 2196, South Africa

Penguin Books Ltd, Registered Offices: 80 Strand, London WC2R 0RL, England

www.penguin.com

First published 2000
10

Made and printed in England by Clays Ltd, St Ives plc

British Library Cataloguing in Publication Data
A CIP catalogue record for this book is available from the British Library

ISBN 0–141–30742–0

Contents

1. All About Harry

Harry is the most annoying younger brother in the entire universe.

For a start, he's always going into my bedroom, especially when I'm not there. I'll come home and find he's left all my computer games out everywhere. Or he's taken something out of my bedroom without even asking – the other day, he took my beanbag away and chucked it downstairs. Then Mum tripped over it and started having a go at me. He thought that was so funny.

He's also really noisy and he wakes me up at night. His bedroom is right next to mine. So in the middle of the night, I'll hear him playing his story tapes or searching through his drawers for one of his games. Sometimes he'll even call my name out. 'Jamie, Jamie,' he shouts. If he's awake, I've got to be awake too.

But the worst thing of all – and this is a bit embarrassing – is that I'm two years and three months older than Harry, but he's taller than me. Half a head taller. I come up to the middle of his ear.

Of course Harry just loves being taller than me. And when someone mistakes him for the older one of us – well, he'll smile about that for days afterwards. It isn't fair, is it? I shouldn't have to look up to my little brother.

I don't tell anyone how badly I feel about this – except Reema. She lives in the road next to mine and she's my best friend. One time when I was complaining, Reema suggested I just ignore Harry, act as if he wasn't really there.

I tried this. Whenever Harry came near me, I just closed my eyes and hummed to myself. But then he punched me, so I had to punch him back in self-defence, didn't I? Then we started having this massive fight until Mum came in and stopped us.

Guess whose fault it was? I'm the older one, so I should set an example.

Anyway, just when I thought my brother couldn't get any worse, there came a bombshell. I'd gone round to

Reema's house after school. When I got back, Mum, Dad and Harry were looking so happy I thought we must have won the lottery at least.

Mum said, 'Good news, Jamie. We've just heard Harry is going to be in the borough sports. He's passed the trials for the school's sports day. He will be their youngest competitor.'

Mum and Dad were dead proud, I could see that. But I just thought, why

wasn't it me? I'd entered the trials too. Dad must have realized what I was thinking because he said, 'It'll be your turn next, Jamie.'

I didn't answer. My eyes were burning and my throat had gone very dry.

Then Mum said, very quietly, 'You should say well done to your brother.'

I glanced up. There was Harry waiting for me to say it, looking all smug and pleased with himself. He knew he could run faster than me and jump higher. He had it all.

It wasn't fair.

And I couldn't say well done to him. Instead I bolted out of the house.

I heard Dad calling me.

'I'm going back round Reema's,' I cried, and didn't wait for him to reply.

When I got to Reema's house, Mrs

Patel said, 'Oh, you've just missed her. She's gone to tea with her nan. Can I give her a message?'

'It's all right, thanks,' I mumbled.

I didn't want to go home. So instead I wandered into the wood opposite my house. I wasn't supposed to go in there without telling Mum or Dad first.

I walked along with my head down, muttering, 'Why do all the good things happen to my brother? I wish something really exciting would happen to me for a change.'

Then I looked up and started in amazement.

You won't believe what I saw …

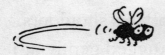

2. An Amazing Discovery

High in the branches of a tree hung a dark blue cape. It seemed to have just landed there. I wanted to get a closer look, so I jumped on to the lowest branch and started pulling myself up. Now I could see there were bright gold stars all around the sides of the cape. And just inside the collar was the number seven. This was gold too and shone as if it had just been polished.

But where had it come from? A parachute might suddenly appear on the top of a tree, but not a cape. Unless – unless a magician had been flying through the air in such a hurry the cape had slipped off his shoulders.

The wind tugged gently at it. I wouldn't have been surprised if the cape had soared off into the sky again. I climbed nearer. All at once, I could reach out and touch it. My hands began to tingle. Maybe a magician was searching for his missing cape at this very moment.

Should I leave it where it was? But I couldn't do that. So instead, I tugged the cape off the branches and very carefully carried it back down to the ground. I felt as if I'd found treasure.

I searched for a name or a label. There was none. The inside of the cape was black velvet. It felt soft and silky. It also looked brand new, as if it had come straight out of the shops. But right then, I knew my cape hadn't come from any shop.

I put it around my shoulders. Immediately, a shiver ran through me, and I suddenly felt lighter too, as if I could fly all the way home. I didn't. But

my feet hardly seemed to touch the ground.

I raced into the kitchen, grinning all over my face. Mum, Dad and Harry were sitting round the table.

'We've already finished eating,' said Mum. 'So next time you go round to Reema's …' she stopped. 'Wherever did you get that from?'

'I found it hanging from a tree,' I replied.

'You've been to the woods without telling us,' said Dad.

He looked across at Mum, but she was still gazing at my cape. 'It's beautiful,' she murmured.

Then Harry touched it.

'Hands off,' I muttered.

'It's too big for you,' he said.

'No it's not. It fits me perfectly … and

it's nothing to do with you,' I added.

'I want one,' cried Harry. 'It's not fair, Jamie's got a cape and I haven't.'

'Sorry,' I said, smiling. 'There's only one cape like this in the whole world, and it belongs to me.'

'Are you sure you found it hanging in a tree?' asked Dad.

'Yes,' I said indignantly.

'Well I don't know if you can keep it, love. Someone must be missing that,' said Mum.

'But if no one *is* missing it, then it's mine?' I asked.

'We'll see,' said Mum.

Mum put up a notice in the post office. For a while, I lived in dread of someone knocking on the door and claiming my cape, but no one ever did. Mum said it was all a bit of a mystery, but in the end she agreed that I could keep it.

I wore the cape everywhere, even sometimes to school. My magician's cape, as I called it. I let Reema try it on. She thought it was brilliant. She was fascinated by the number seven on the collar.

'Seven's supposed to be a magic number,' she said, 'so that's a little sign your cape is very special.'

She and I pretended the cape could do magic. So if a teacher told us off for talking, I'd put my left thumb (I am left-handed) on the seven and whisper, 'I want you to turn that horrible teacher into a rhinoceros right now.' Nothing ever happened, but the idea still made Reema and me burst out laughing.

Of course, I put spells on Harry. I'd get

my cape to turn him into all sorts of
animals – and I'd often make him
invisible too. My spells might not have
worked, but I enjoyed making them. And
I felt different when I was wearing that
cape: bigger, stronger, more powerful.

I was certain that one day my cape
would do something magical. And one
day it did.

3. The Missing Cape

The magic happened on Saturday 7th
July.

The day started really badly. I woke up
and discovered my cape had gone.

I'd put it over the chair as usual, but
now it had vanished. Maybe my cape had
just flown away. Anything seemed
possible. I bunged on a shirt and trousers
and tore downstairs. I could hear Mum

and Dad's voices – and Aunt Nora's too.

Why was she here so early? Then I remembered. It was Mum and Dad's anniversary today. They were going out for a special lunch, and Aunt Nora would be looking after us.

I burst out, 'My cape, it's gone!'

Three startled faces turned towards me.

'Of course it hasn't gone,' said Dad.

Aunt Nora jumped up and gave me one of her sloppy kisses. She was actually my mum's aunt, so she was incredibly ancient. 'How are you, dear?' she asked.

'He hasn't brushed his hair yet,' began Mum.

What did my hair matter at a time like this? 'My cape's gone,' I repeated.

'You've left it somewhere downstairs,' said Mum.

'No, I haven't,' I cried. But I dashed off

and checked while Mum and Dad gave embarrassed laughs and said, 'He just loves that cape.'

I sprang around the sitting room, searching under piles of magazines and books. Then I happened to glance out of the window. The next moment I let out a cry of anger, pushed open the back door and charged outside. It was raining, but I didn't care. All I saw was my brother prancing about in my cape, chanting, 'I'm a magician and I can do magic.'

I ran over to him, my slippers sloshing about on the grass and shouted, 'How dare you go into my room and take my cape!'

'I would have asked you, but you were asleep,' Harry shouted back.

'Well give it back.' I made to pull it off him, but Harry darted away.

'I haven't finished with it yet,' he cried.

'Yes, you have!' I yelled, so loudly that he stopped.

'There's no need …' he began. But before he could say any more, I'd pulled the cape away from him.

I held it up triumphantly. But it was wet and streaked with mud. 'Look what you've done to it!' I cried.

Suddenly, a deep voice bellowed, 'Stop making all that noise!' It made us both jump. The voice seemed to come from

17

nowhere. Then I realized it was our next-door neighbour, Mr Granger.

He glared over the fence at us, breathing heavily, raindrops dribbling down his nose. 'I can hear you inside my house!' he cried. 'What's the matter with the pair of you? There's no discipline today. That's the problem ...'

He moaned on, while I examined all the dirt on my precious cape. After he'd gone, I put my thumb on the number and whispered, 'Number Seven, turn Mr Granger into a dragon.'

Then Harry jumped on me and we both fell in the mud. 'I only want to borrow it,' he hissed in my ear.

'You're not getting it ever!' I cried. Harry was bigger and stronger than me, but I was determined to hold on to my cape.

We started fighting. I don't know who would have won, because we suddenly heard a voice say, 'Stop this at once.'

It was Mum, her face dark with rage. 'Just look at the pair of you!' she exclaimed.

We staggered to our feet. I tried to explain what had happened, but Harry kept interrupting.

'You're both to blame,' said Mum. 'But you should know better, Jamie.'

After we'd washed and got changed, we were sent to our bedrooms. Mum and Dad left for their anniversary meal in a very bad mood. They told Aunt Nora we could come downstairs for our lunch – as Reema was coming round then – but not a second before.

I sat in my room, furious that I was in trouble again because of my brother.

Still, at least I had got my cape back,
even if it was all splattered with mud. I
crept into the bathroom and washed the
mud off. I'd just finished when I heard a
voice behind me. 'What are you doing?'

I didn't even bother to turn round.
'Mind your own business, Harry.' I put
the cape round my shoulders. 'And leave
my things alone.'

Harry came closer, towering over me. 'Sorry, Jamie,' he said. He put one hand on my shoulder. 'I didn't mean …'

I shook his hand away. He was really bugging me today. I was sick of him buzzing around me all the time. He was like one of those really noisy flies. You know, bluebottles. They won't leave you alone, especially if you've got food, and they keep flying into you.

I found the number seven on the collar, slammed my thumb down on it and hissed, 'Number Seven, please turn Harry, the most annoying person I know, into the most annoying bug I know: a bluebottle.'

Harry heard me, looked hurt and, without another word, left. Well, serve him right.

Suddenly Harry called out my name

from the landing. He sounded as though he was standing on a chair or something, because his voice came from really high up. Another of his pathetic tricks.

I ignored him. Then suddenly, I heard this loud, buzzing noise, the sound a bee makes or a ...

I whirled round.

A bluebottle came flying towards me.

4. Bug Brother

I shook my head in disbelief. I hadn't
really turned my brother into a
bluebottle. He was hiding somewhere.
One of his silly jokes.

Well, I wasn't going to fall for that one.
I walked back to my room, whistling
loudly. Then, as my cape was still a bit
wet, I put the hairdryer on it. I was
whistling even louder now.

But there was no sign of Harry. That bluebottle was still circling around me though. It never left me alone. It seemed really worked up.

I ran into Harry's bedroom. I looked under the bed, opened the wardrobe. Then I checked Mum and Dad's room. He certainly wasn't upstairs. I went downstairs. I saw Aunt Nora busy in the kitchen. But no one else. And everywhere I went, that bluebottle followed behind.

I rushed back to my bedroom. And the bluebottle came too. I gaped at it, horrified, yet excited too. I'd wished for my brother to be a bluebottle, and somehow the wish had come true. It must be the cape. It really *was* magic. This was totally incredible.

I couldn't wait to tell Reema. The smile on my face just grew and grew. I was very happy. But the bluebottle wasn't. He was buzzing furiously round and round my head. Only my brother could make that much noise.

'All right, just calm down, Harry,' I said. 'And stop flying around my head. You're making me feel dizzy.'

The bluebottle slowed down.

'I'm sorry about what's happened. I know it must have been a bit of a shock for you. But don't worry, I'll turn you back. No problem.' Then I paused. 'Of course, if I turn you back, you do promise never to take anything from my room again?'

The bluebottle was suddenly completely silent. I took that to mean, Yes.

'And do you promise not to be so annoying in future?'

25

All at once the bluebottle alighted on my nose. I could see him properly now. There was a flash of blue on his body and two midget antennae coming out of his head. I liked his little wings best. They were swish, but were vibrating anxiously. I think he wanted me to hurry up. I'd never known my brother get so worked up. I'd tease him about this afterwards.

I put the cape on and held my thumb on the number seven. I was certain this was the really magic part. I said loudly, 'Number Seven, I want you to turn my brother back into his normal shape again.' Then I waited.

But nothing happened. I couldn't believe it. Harry was still perched on my nose.

'I'll try again,' I whispered. 'Perhaps I need to say the words a bit slower.'

So I wished more slowly and *still* nothing happened.

I had a third go, pressing the number seven really heavily. This time something *did* happen. The bluebottle started dive-bombing me, flying towards me from all different angles.

'Hey, stop it. I'm doing my best.'

Then Aunt Nora called, 'All right, boys, you can come downstairs; I'm serving up now.'

My heart began to thump. How could I explain to Aunt Nora what had happened? I couldn't. The shock might kill her.

The doorbell rang. 'Jamie, that'll be your friend. Answer it, will you?' asked Aunt Nora from the kitchen.

I turned to the bluebottle. 'Look, just wait here, all right?'

I rushed downstairs and opened the
front door. I saw Reema grinning
cheerfully at me. Then I let out a cry of
horror as the bluebottle flew past me and
disappeared straight out of the door.

'Follow that bluebottle,' I shouted.

'Why?' cried Reema.

'I'll explain later, just follow it!' I shot
off down the road.

Reema came panting after me. 'Is this some kind of joke?'

'No,' I gasped, then yelled, 'You're being really stupid! Stop now.'

'What?' cried Reema.

'It's all right; I'm not talking to you.'

'Who are you talking to?'

'That bluebottle,' I gasped.

'Of course you are,' she murmured.

Suddenly the bluebottle dived into someone's front garden. I sprinted after him.

Reema tugged my arm. 'But we can't just go into people's gardens.'

'We've no choice,' I said. I watched the bluebottle fly on to the rooftop. 'Oh great,' I snapped.

'Jamie, what is going on?' demanded Reema.

I turned to her. 'I wished on my cape

for Harry to be a bluebottle and it came true. But I can't change him back.'

'What are you talking about?' she gasped.

Well, I didn't see how I could have put it much clearer. I started to explain again, but this time she interrupted me.

'So that bluebottle really is Harry?' Her eyes were as wide as a car's headlamps.

I nodded.

'But that's so amazing.' She gave Harry a little wave. 'Hi there, Harry,' she hissed.

One of the upstairs windows opened. A smartly dressed woman scowled down at us. 'Yes, what do you want?'

'Er, er, what we wanted was …' But my brain just seized up. I turned to Reema for help.

'We're looking for someone called Harry and wondered if you'd seen him,' said Reema.

'Why would I have seen him?' asked the woman.

'Because he's sitting on your roof,' I murmured. That made Reema giggle nervously.

'What does Harry look like?' demanded the woman.

At that moment, Harry took off again.

'It's all right, we've found him,' cried Reema. 'Bye.'

The woman banged the window shut while Harry streaked off in the opposite direction.

'Maybe he's going back,' said Reema.

'I hope so,' I replied.

Reema and I chased after him all the way home. Then he flew over our gate and disappeared off in the direction of the back garden.

Aunt Nora was waiting in the doorway. 'Oh, there you are. Everything's all ready. How are you, Reema?'

Reema was too puffed to answer. She could only smile and nod.

'Where have you been?' asked Aunt Nora.

'We just went for a little walk,' I panted.

'I don't know why you couldn't have waited until after you'd eaten,' said Aunt Nora. 'And where's Harry?'

'Harry?' I cried. 'He's in the back garden.'

'Well, tell him to come inside at once,' said Aunt Nora.

I gulped hard. 'Yeah, right.'

I went into the back garden. The sun

was blazing down and the air was thick with insects. There was a whole team of bees on the clover, while others were busy on the roses and honeysuckle. Butterflies flitted nervously past them while two wasps hovered menacingly outside our shed in their striped football jerseys. But where was Harry?

I couldn't see him anywhere. 'Harry,' I hissed. 'Come on, I want to help you.' Finally I heard this loud buzz coming from the apple tree. I looked up. Harry was reclining on a large leaf.

He lay there, buzzing furiously.

'I don't blame you being mad, Harry, but I'll get you out of this soon. I promise.'

'Jamie, Harry,' called Aunt Nora. 'Hurry up.'

I whispered, 'I've got to go, but I'll be

back, so just stay where you are, and …
enjoy the view.'

I tore back into the house. Aunt Nora
and Reema had already started eating. I
sat down.

Aunt Nora peered at me through her
glasses. 'But where's Harry?'

'He's still outside,' I said. 'He's hiding.'

'What nonsense,' declared Aunt Nora.
She marched into the sitting room,
opened the window and called, 'Harry,
come inside now. Hurry up.' She sat
down again. 'It's not like Harry to miss a
meal. He loves his food.' She sounded a
bit anxious.

'I'm sure he'll come in soon,' said
Reema.

Then the phone rang. Luckily it was
Aunt Nora's daughter, Susan. Soon she
was gabbling away.

Reema leant forward. 'So where's Harry?'

'Sunbathing on the apple tree.'

'You can't leave him out there. Anything might happen to him. He might get eaten.'

'Who'd want to eat him?' I replied. But actually, I was worried too. 'I'll get him to come inside.'

I ran back to the apple tree. He hadn't moved. 'Harry, get into the house, will you?'

He gave a little buzz as if to say, 'No, I won't.'

'Look, I want to help you, but I can't with you stuck out here. So do what I tell you and get inside, now.'

He buzzed quite loudly this time.

'You're so annoying,' I cried.

With that, I rushed into the shed and came out brandishing Dad's fishing net.

My brother couldn't escape me now. I stole up towards him, swung the net into the air and pounced.

Then I heard a triumphant hum above my head and watched Harry soaring up into the sky.

'Get back here now,' I yelled. 'Harry, if you don't come back right now you're going to be very sorry.' But I was talking to myself. He'd gone.

'Even when he's a bluebottle you're fighting with him.'

I spun round to see Reema frowning at me.

'It's Harry's fault. Would you believe it? He's just taken off!' I exclaimed.

'I don't blame him,' said Reema.

'What?'

'Why should he listen to you? You've turned him into a bluebottle. You've ruined his life.'

'Look, I never meant this to happen.'
My voice fell. 'What am I going to do
now?'

'We've got to get him back inside. Then
at least we'll know he's not been
swallowed by a bird or …'

'And how do we do that?' I interrupted.

Reema paused, then smiled. 'I think
I've just had a brilliant idea.'

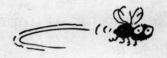

5. Where's Harry?

I thought Reema's idea was brilliant too. We quickly set about carrying it out. Aunt Nora was still gabbling away on the phone, so she didn't see me creep into the kitchen and bring out a new jar of strawberry jam and two large spoons.

'Harry must be starving by now,' said Reema. 'And bluebottles like jam more than anything. He won't be able to resist this.'

We began scooping it over the step. 'We'll need to put a lot down,' said Reema, 'so that he can smell it.'

It didn't take long for us to practically empty the whole jar.

Soon we had our first visitor: a wasp.

'Clear off,' cried Reema. 'This isn't for you.'

But the wasp seemed hypnotized by the jam and wouldn't go away.

'All right, help yourself,' I hissed to the wasp. 'Just don't tell your friends about the free food.'

I stood and waited behind the door, with my net, ready for Reema's signal. 'Any sign of Harry?' I whispered.

'No, but that wasp is still here and we've got a couple of flies too.'

Then, all at once, Reema let out a cry and started running up the garden.

I leapt out of my hiding place. 'What's happened?'

'That wasp tried to sting me,' she said. 'He's definitely not getting any more jam now.'

Moments later, Reema whispered, 'I see him.'

I darted forward and before the bluebottle knew what was happening, I'd caught him. 'Gotcha!' I cried, racing upstairs with him. I sprang into my bedroom, slamming the door behind me. I checked all my windows were shut too.

'Now, Harry, I need to explain something to you. I want to help you. But I can't if you keep flying off. So for your own safety, I'm going to keep you in here and try to turn you back to normal. All right?'

The bluebottle didn't answer. It was flying around the room, but silently.

'You're not sulking, are you? Buzz once so I know you're still talking to me.'

But the bluebottle refused to buzz at all.

I squinted at him. 'You *are* Harry, aren't you?' He seemed smaller than Harry, and much duller in colour. And he didn't fly around me or make any noises. He just hid behind the curtains.

I groaned with frustration: I felt a bit silly having spent the last few minutes chatting to a bluebottle.

Reema was waiting for me back out in the garden. Every wasp and fly in the area was now feasting on the jam.

'How's Harry?' she asked.

I shook my head. 'It's not him.'

'How do you know?'

'I know my own brother.' I gave a deep sigh. 'He could be miles away by now.'

Just then, Aunt Nora appeared. She gazed in horror at all the jam on the step. 'Whatever have you been doing, Jamie?'

'It was an experiment, Aunt Nora,' I mumbled. 'We wanted to see which insects liked jam.'

'It's been really interesting,' added Reema.

'But what a mess you've made!' cried my aunt. 'And you've attracted such horrible creatures. We've got to clean it up.'

We helped Aunt Nora wash down the step. Suddenly she asked, 'And where's Harry?'

'Oh, he's around,' I replied. 'I think he's hiding again.'

'He's been very naughty today,' said Aunt Nora. 'Just wait until I see him.' She looked around to try and spot him. 'Such a beautiful garden,' she continued. 'All it lacks are a few garden gnomes. I think they bring such character to a garden.'

Personally, I've always thought garden gnomes were a bit silly. They always have such daft expressions on their faces. But I was polite and agreed with her.

'Well,' she went on, 'your mother promised I could help myself to a few cuttings, so I'll do that now. You can run along and play, but don't make any more mess. And tell Harry I want to see him, will you?'

'We will,' I promised.

Back inside I said, 'What are we going to do now?'

Reema frowned. 'I'm not sure.'

'I don't know why my cape can turn Harry into a bluebottle – but not back again.'

'Maybe the cape only grants one wish a day,' suggested Reema.

'Or it could just be a one-wish cape,' I said gloomily.

'Or perhaps,' said Reema softly, 'you

just don't want Harry back enough.'

I looked up sharply. 'What do you mean?'

'Well, you're always moaning about him.'

'Yes,' I agreed. 'And he is totally annoying. But …'

'Yes?' asked Reema.

'Well, he's still my brother and I *do* want him back.' I whispered those last words as if I were admitting a terrible secret. Then I looked at my watch. It was four o'clock. 'About now he'd be getting ready to watch the last episode of *Thief in Time*. He hasn't missed an episode. He sits right up close to the screen when it's on …'

I stopped. I looked at Reema. We both had the same idea at the same time. I jumped up and switched the television on and turned up the volume as loud as I could while Reema rushed around, opening every window.

The theme music of *Thief in Time* boomed out of the TV. Aunt Nora was still in the garden and luckily her hearing wasn't very good anyway.

'I'm sure if he hears that music he'll fly in,' I said. 'He's desperate to know what happens at the end.'

'Fingers crossed then,' said Reema.

I went into the kitchen and found an empty jam jar. I explained, 'When we catch him, I'll keep him in here. Then at least I'll know he's safe. I'll just make some air holes in the lid.'

I'd just finished, when I heard a familiar buzzing noise. A bluebottle started circling around the room. Then it settled on the television screen.

'That's my brother all right.' I gave a massive sigh of relief.

Reema looked really pleased too. 'Talk to him,' she hissed. 'Go on, make up.'

I edged towards the bluebottle, which was sitting dead still, right in the middle of the television screen. I crouched down. 'Sorry to interrupt your favourite programme, but I need to put you inside this jam jar. There's lots of space and six air holes …'

At once the bluebottle began whirling round and round my head, making more noise than a swarm of angry bees.

'I don't think he likes that idea,' began Reema.

I looked up at Harry. 'All right, just stop doing that, will you?'

'There's no point in shouting at him,' said Reema. 'He'll only fly away again.'

I took a deep breath. 'Harry, calm
down. You needn't go into the jam jar if
you don't want to. What would you like
to do?'

He began flying around the TV screen.

'Oh, look!' cried Reema. 'He wants to
watch his favourite programme in peace.
You can't stop him doing that.'

She turned to the bluebottle. 'You go
on enjoying your TV programme. You'll
be perfectly safe, I promise.'

The bluebottle scuttled across the screen a few times before settling himself down again.

'See, he's fine now,' whispered Reema.

After the programme had finished I leant forward and spoke to the bluebottle. 'I want to help you, Harry.'

Immediately his wings started to vibrate.

I turned to Reema. 'Why won't he trust me?'

'Well you did turn him into a bluebottle,' replied Reema, 'so you can't blame him for being a *bit* suspicious.'

'I suppose so.' Then I whispered, 'Reema, what am I going to do if I can't turn him back?'

The bluebottle's wings were vibrating very fast now.

'You're upsetting him again,' whispered

Reema. She went over to Harry. 'Now, are you hungry?'

He made a loud buzzing noise.

'Well, there's still a little jam left, so follow me.'

Harry didn't need any more prompting. He flew off to the kitchen with Reema.

I was about to follow them when I had an idea. I ran upstairs to the bathroom. Then I flicked some water on to my cape. You see, I'd just remembered something. When I'd turned Harry into a bluebottle, the cape had been a bit wet. Afterwards, I'd dried it with the hairdryer. Was that why my wishes weren't coming true any more? Did the seven on my cape need to be wet before it could do any magic? I was certain that was the solution.

Suddenly, I heard Reema scream. 'Jamie, come quickly.'

6. Aunt Nora Vanishes

I sped downstairs, the cape still in my hand. Then I exclaimed in horror.

My aunt was chasing Harry around the kitchen with a massive fly swat. 'These flies carry so many germs,' she cried.

'But this bluebottle doesn't!' screamed Reema. 'Please stop.'

'They cause nothing but harm,

especially in the kitchen,' replied Aunt Nora. She lunged forward with the fly swat and actually hit Harry.

Harry went shooting off around the room, with Aunt Nora close behind.

Reema spotted me in the doorway. 'Jamie, *do* something!' she shrieked.

'Aunt Nora,' I began. But I could see this wasn't the moment to reason with her.

Now she was taking aim again. And Harry was too stunned to get out of her way. A terrible shudder ran through me. I squeezed the cape and cried, 'Number Seven, please turn Aunt Nora into a … a garden gnome.'

Aunt Nora turned to me in utter astonishment. 'What did you say, Jamie?'

Reema saw her chance. 'Harry, quick!' she cried. She tore open the door and fled outside, with Harry close behind.

And then the oddest thing happened.
Aunt Nora began to rise up into the air. It
was just as if she was climbing up an
invisible escalator. She went up higher
and higher. Soon she was touching the
ceiling.

She turned her head to look down at me. 'Jamie, what's … er, happening?'

Before I could reply, her body gave a little twist and vanished.

I just stood there, swallowing hard.

Reema rushed in. 'Harry's outside. I told him to wait by the apple tree. He still looks pretty dazed. Where's Aunt Nora gone?'

'I'm not sure,' I began. 'But I think we should go for a little stroll in the garden.'

Reema and I went outside.

Then we both nearly jumped out of our skin. It was the shock of suddenly seeing a garden gnome right in the middle of the lawn. In the gnome's hand was a fishing rod. As we got nearer, we saw the gnome's face.

That gave us the biggest shock of all, for smiling away at us was *Aunt Nora*.

7. Harry in Danger

Reema and I walked round and round Aunt Nora. She was still wearing her glasses.

'She looks so weird,' said Reema, 'but kind of happy too. At least you know your cape's working again.'

'All it needed was a bit of watering. The magic only seems to happen when the cape's wet.' I crouched down. 'Hey, look! Aunt Nora's still breathing.'

'So she is. Do you think she can hear us?'

'Maybe.' I moved nearer to her. 'Aunt Nora, I just wanted to apologize for turning you into a garden gnome. Hope it wasn't too much of a shock for you. But you've always liked garden gnomes, haven't you?' I stopped. 'No, I don't think she can hear me.'

Certainly there was no reaction from Aunt Nora. She was completely still, except for her shoulders, which moved very slightly every time she breathed in and out. So I just gave her a friendly little pat and said, 'Sorry for the inconvenience.'

'It's probably quite restful being a garden gnome for a little while,' said Reema.

'And I'll turn her back soon. But first we've got to find Harry.'

We ran to the apple tree where Reema had told him to wait. He was nowhere to be seen.

'Oh why won't he ever do what he's told,' I cried. 'Where's he gone off to now?'

Suddenly, we heard a loud snorting noise. It came from next-door's garden and made us both jump.

'Your neighbour's got a terrible cold,' said Reema. 'What's his name?'

'Mr Granger,' I replied absently. But it was Harry I was thinking about.

Moments later, I heard something else. 'Reema, listen.'

'What?'

'Don't you hear it? A buzzing noise, only it's really faint.'

'I can't hear a thing.' She looked at me. 'Do you think it's Harry?'

'It doesn't sound like him. But we'd
better trail it just the same.' Straining our
ears, we followed the noise round to the
back gate. Three bins were lined up
against the wall. A stale smell always
hovered over them.

And then I saw something that turned
my blood to icicles.

A spider's web was stretched right
across one wall. And trapped
right in the middle
of it ... was
Harry.

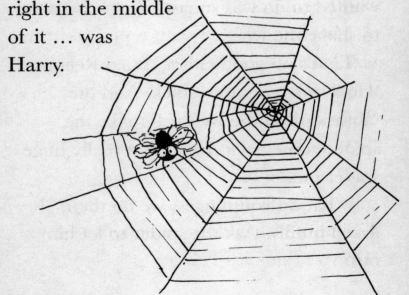

Reema gasped with horror. 'Oh no, poor little Harry.'

He wriggled his legs and gave another sad, frightened buzz.

Immediately, I tried to pull him out.

'No, don't do that!' screeched Reema. 'You could tear his wings or pull one of his legs off.'

'Oh, all right.' She'd scared me a bit yelling like that, but the last thing I wanted to do was squash Harry. I started to shake the web.

'That's no good either,' cried Reema. 'He'll only get more stuck. And the vibrations on the web will make the spider come back. I bet it's a really huge spider too.'

'What do you suggest we do then?' I asked huffily. 'Ask the spider to let him out?'

'Get a spoon.'

'A spoon,' I repeated. I had to admit that was a really good idea. I tore into the kitchen, pulled a large spoon out of the drawer and dashed back.

Reema was crouched down and whispering to Harry. 'Please stop twitching your legs. It'll only get you more tangled.'

'Don't panic, Harry,' I said. 'We'll soon have you out of this torture chamber. I'm armed now,' I added, waving the spoon in the air.

I started pulling away at the web. It felt silky and sticky, like really thin bubblegum and was wound tightly around Harry's body. But I slowly unpicked it, bit by bit.

Reema was watching me keenly. 'Right, get Harry out now.'

I reached forward with the spoon. But bits of the web were still sticking to Harry like glue.

'Be careful!' screeched Reema.

'I am.'

'He's very delicate, you know.'

'My brother, delicate?' I muttered. 'Never.' But my hand was starting to shake.

'Steady, steady,' I murmured to myself. And then in one quick movement, I scooped Harry up. Tiny fragments of the web still clung to him, and he was sitting very still, but he was free.

I felt quite wobbly with relief, but hid it by trying to say something funny. 'There we are,' I joked, holding out the spoon, 'one helping of bluebottle. Would you like anything on it?'

'He's not moving!' cried Reema.

But all at once he *did* move. He

fluttered off the spoon and on to my
hand.

'Aaah, look at that,' cried Reema. 'He
wants to be with his big brother. Well,
you did stop him from being a spider's
dinner.' She studied Harry. 'I think he's
still in shock,' she whispered.

I blew gently on him and watched the
last pieces of the web fall away. I said,
'Cheer up, little bug brother, I've got my

cape working again, so I can definitely change you back.'

Some of his buzz returned when he heard that.

'I just need to wet the cape, Harry, and then …' Before I could say anything else, the doorbell rang.

We dashed to the front door, with Harry still on my hand. I gazed through the peephole and then gulped. Mum and Dad were home!

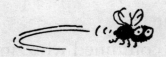

8. Something Incredible

I looked at Reema. 'It's my parents. We can't let them in. If they see Aunt Nora and Harry, it'll …'

'Ruin their anniversary,' interrupted Reema. 'I'll just have to keep them talking while you change everyone back. But be quick, won't you?'

'I'll be like lightning. Only faster!' Harry was skimming about excitedly.

You could tell he was really eager to see Mum and Dad.

'Harry, you can't see them right now,' I said. 'They won't recognize you anyhow. So go upstairs to your room and I'll come up in a minute.'

But Harry continued whizzing around the hall. I knew I'd never be able to catch him. He knew that too.

Then Dad called through the letterbox. 'Hello, we've forgotten our key. Is anyone about or shall we just pop round the back?'

That made Reema and I spring into the air with horror. They couldn't go round the back. They'd spot Aunt Nora right away. Well, you couldn't exactly miss her.

I looked up at Harry. 'Harry, trust me and go up to your bedroom, now, please.'

Harry stopped. He seemed to be

66

considering what I'd just said. Then he gave a buzz as if to say, 'Don't be long,' and slowly flew upstairs.

'Thanks, Harry, I won't let you down,' I whispered as I opened the front door.

'At last,' said Mum. But she was smiling. Both she and Dad seemed to be in an exceptionally good mood. Mum was carrying an enormous bunch of flowers. 'Have you been behaving yourself for Aunt Nora?' she asked.

'Oh yes,' I said. 'She's in the garden. I'll go and get her for you.'

'It's all right, I'll come with you,' began Mum.

But Reema suddenly yelled, 'Oh, what lovely flowers!'

Both Mum and Dad stepped back in alarm.

'Oh, please may I hold them?' Reema continued.

'Yes, all right, dear,' said Mum, looking startled.

'Oh, aren't they beautiful,' gushed Reema. 'Now you must tell me what each flower is called.'

I zoomed off into the kitchen and flicked some water on to my cape. Then I charged into the garden. Aunt Nora was still quietly fishing. I grabbed hold of the cape and wished. 'Number Seven, please turn Aunt Nora back into her normal self again.'

At first, nothing happened. I began to

count softly to myself. I'd reached seven
when the garden gnome shot up
into the air like a rocket.

The next moment, it
had vanished and there
was Aunt
Nora, sitting
on the
grass. She
rubbed
her eyes,
then looked
up at me. 'But how
extraordinary! I must have dozed off for
a minute.' She stretched.

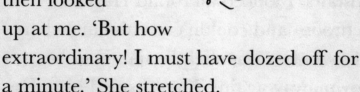

'Mum and Dad are back, Aunt Nora.'

'Are they? Right.' Aunt Nora sprang to
her feet. 'That little nap's done me a
power of good.' And she walked so
quickly into the house I had to run to

keep up with her.

Mum and Dad were still trapped in the doorway, thanks to Reema. She was saying, 'I know you told me before, but what's this lovely flower called again?'

Then Mum spotted Aunt Nora. She rushed forward. 'There you are, is everything all right?'

'Yes, splendid,' said Aunt Nora, beaming. 'I've never felt better.'

I gave Reema a quick grin, then flew upstairs. I looked all round Harry's bedroom and couldn't see him anywhere. My window was slightly ajar. Had he flown away again? Then I spied him. He was walking upside down along the ceiling. You'd never have guessed he'd only been a bluebottle for an afternoon.

I thought then, if bluebottles ever hold athletic competitions, I bet my brother

could win every prize and I felt a flicker
of jealousy, which I quickly brushed away.
Especially as Harry seemed so pleased to
see me. He flew around me, buzzing
happily.

'Harry, I'm going to change you back,
right now.' I gripped hold of the cape
and said, 'Number Seven, please turn
Harry back to his normal shape.'

After a couple of seconds, Harry's
wings began to quiver. 'Don't panic,' I
said, 'the magic takes seven seconds. I've
timed it.'

And sure enough, on the seventh
second, the bluebottle whizzed right up to
the ceiling. The next moment, it had
disappeared and there, curled up on the
bed, was the familiar shape of my brother.
His eyes were shut. Then they sprang
open. He sat up, staring all around him.

'I've been dreaming,' he said, in this funny, blurred voice, 'a really weird dream.' He was quivering like a blancmange.

'Are you all right?' I asked.

'Yeah, of course I am,' he said fiercely. Then he flopped down on the bed again.

'Mum and Dad are back,' I said. He didn't answer. 'Are you coming downstairs then?' I asked.

'Not yet.' His voice was small and tight. Something was wrong here. I wanted to stay. But I didn't know what else to say. You see, I never ever chatted with my brother; I just rowed with him. So I left and bumped into Reema. 'Harry's back,' I said.

Reema let out a great sigh of relief but then she cried, 'Jamie, there's something you've got to see.'

I stared at her. 'Aunt Nora hasn't

changed back, has she?'

'Just follow me,' replied Reema. 'And hurry.'

I followed Reema into the garden. 'So what's the big mystery?' I asked.

Reema pointed. 'Just take a look over that fence.' Then her voice started to shake. 'But don't let him see you.'

I knew Mr Granger could be very fierce. But I was surprised to see Reema looking quite so scared. I climbed to the top of the fence and peered into Mr Granger's garden. It was always so neat and boring. Then suddenly I saw something really incredible. Sitting in a deckchair was a bright green dragon.

9. The Seventh Wish

The dragon was reading a newspaper. It was clamped between its claws, only the bottom part of the newspaper was all singed. Then I realized why. Every time the dragon breathed, black smoke poured out of his nose.

Suddenly, I lost my balance and tumbled on to the grass. Reema helped me up.

'I d … don't believe it,' I stuttered.

'I didn't either at first,' said Reema. 'I heard that snorting noise again, so I peeped over the fence and there it was, a real-life dragon. Luckily he was reading, so he didn't spot me.' Her voice rose. 'Where did that dragon come from, Jamie?'

'How do I know?' I began. And then I remembered. 'Oh no!'

'What?'

'This morning Mr Granger was moaning at us again. So I wished he'd turn into a dragon. I only said it under my breath though.'

'But the cape must have heard.'

'Yeah, and he's been a dragon ever since.' I shook my head in amazement. 'Do you suppose he knows?'

Reema giggled. 'Well just wait until he looks in the mirror.'

'A definite improvement, I'd say.'

We were both grinning now. Then we heard this roaring noise from next door and stopped grinning.

'He could go rampaging off at any moment,' said Reema. 'You've got to turn him back.'

'I know.'

We both clambered to the top of the fence again. The dragon was flinging his newspaper to the ground. It was completely singed now. Then he spotted us and immediately snorted with fury.

'Being a dragon hasn't improved his temper,' I muttered.

'Just get on with it,' whispered Reema.

I grabbed the cape. Luckily it was still wet. I said, 'Number Seven, I wish Mr Granger would turn back into his normal appearance, only, from now on, he will

like all children and never mind if their ball goes into his garden.'

Reema nudged me. 'Oh no,' she gasped. The dragon was charging towards us and now real flames of fire were shooting out of its nose.

'In seven seconds he'll be gone,' I whispered. But the seven seconds seemed to pass very slowly. He came pounding right up to the fence. I could feel the hotness of his smoky breath. Any moment now he was going to smash through into my garden.

Then, all at once, he hurtled backwards, as if he'd just trodden on a banana skin. Next thing, he was high up in the air, roaring and fizzing like a particularly nasty firework.

I waved at him. He must have spotted me because his roaring grew even louder and then he vanished.

'I'm really glad he's gone,' said Reema.

Then we gazed down at Mr Granger sitting on the grass. He got up, spotted the dragon's footsteps on his lawn, and began muttering furiously to himself. Then he noticed how the washing on his line was covered in smoke.

'Someone's let a large dog into my garden,' he called, 'and someone else is having a horrible bonfire. Why are my neighbours so inconsiderate?' He spied us. At once, his face twisted into a smile. 'Why, hello there, children. Good to see you. How are you both?'

It was quite a shock to see Mr Granger being so nice to us. 'We're fine, thanks,' I whispered.

'Good.' He waved to us and then we climbed down from the fence.

'What about that?' I said. 'Hey, are you OK, Reema?'

'Oh, yes, it's just the way that dragon came charging towards us … it was a bit scary.'

I decided Reema needed a long, cool glass of lemonade to calm her nerves. I *was* going to get her one from the kitchen, but I didn't need to go to all that bother. I could wish her a drink. So I said,

'Number Seven, give Reema a large glass
of lemonade please.'

'Oh don't do that!' cried Reema.

'Why not? Don't you want a drink?'

'Yes,' faltered Reema.

Next moment, the biggest glass of
lemonade I'd ever seen appeared beside
her. Reema reached out and took a sip.
'Delicious,' she said. 'Try a bit.'

I did. 'It's great. Still, only the best from the cape.'

'Yes.' Then Reema frowned.

'What is it?' I asked.

'Nothing, only …'

'Go on.'

'Well, I just wondered if your cape has got seven on it because it only grants seven wishes …'

I started. 'And how many wishes have I had?'

'My lemonade was the seventh wish,' she said quietly.

'We'd better wish for something else. I know, I wish that apple tree over there would grow chocolates.'

'That's a silly wish,' said Reema.

'No, it isn't.'

But no chocolates appeared on the tree, or elsewhere. So we tried another wish, this time for a large bar of chocolate. Again, nothing happened.

I stared at Reema in horror. 'You're right. I think I've used all my wishes up.'

Mum came out into the garden. 'Oh, there you are.' She looked curiously at Reema's glass.

'It's mine,' said Reema. 'I brought it to show Jamie.'

'Well, make sure you take care of it,' said Mum. 'It looks valuable.'

Just then, Mr Granger popped his head over the fence. He was holding a ball. 'Excuse me, but is this your ball, Jamie?'

'I'm afraid it is,' began Mum.

Mr Granger glared at her. 'I'm talking to the lad, not you.'

'Yes, it is,' I replied.

Mr Granger's face twisted into another smile. 'There you are, Jamie.' He threw it into the garden. 'And when it comes over again just pop round. You're always welcome. It's good to see young people enjoying themselves.'

Mum could only blink at him in astonishment. 'Well, he's changed, hasn't he?' she said.

'He certainly has,' I replied, winking at Reema.

Then Mum's face became serious. 'Is everything all right with Harry? Did anything happen while I was away?'

'No,' I said quickly. 'Why?'

'Well, he doesn't seem himself,' said Mum.

That gave me a shock. But of course Harry was himself. I'd switched him back.

'He's just sitting in his bedroom,' continued Mum, 'says he doesn't want to come down. I'm not sure why.'

'I'll go and see him,' I began.

Mum looked uneasy. 'Well ...'

'It'll be all right,' I said. I sprinted upstairs. Harry was still lying on his bed. 'Hello.'

'Hello,' he murmured.

'What's wrong?' I asked.

'Nothing.'

'Yes, there is.'

He turned away from me. Then suddenly he blurted out, 'I had a really nasty dream.' He waited for me to burst out laughing.

Instead I leant on the edge of the bed. 'What was it about?' I asked.

'I dreamt you turned me into a bluebottle. I got swatted by Aunt Nora. And then I got stuck in a spider's web. That was really horrible.'

He began to shiver and I actually felt

sorry for my brother. 'It was just a
dream,' I said.

'But it's still in my eyes.' Then he
added, 'In the dream, you rescued me.
You got me out of the spider's web.'

'Did I?' I tried to sound surprised.

'Of course, you wouldn't have done
that really.'

'I might.'

Harry shook his head vigorously. 'You'd
have left me there to be eaten alive.'

'No, I wouldn't.'

'Yes, you would.' His voice rose. 'You'd never help me.'

Harry was getting me cross again. In a minute we'd be arguing. I decided to go. I marched to the door.

Suddenly Harry cried out, 'When I call for you at night you never come.'

I whirled round. 'What are you talking about?'

'I get scared when it's dark,' whispered Harry.

'Do you?' I was totally amazed.

'My bedroom gets really dark sometimes; darker than your room or Mum and Dad's. That's why I call for you.'

All at once, I remembered Harry shouting out at night.

'But I didn't realize. I thought you were

just shouting my name to . . . annoy me.'

'You can never be bothered,' said Harry indignantly.

'Don't be stupid.' I paused. 'Look, next time you need my help, I'll be there.'

His eyes flicked up at me. 'Will you really?'

'Yeah.'

'What about if it's very late?'

'Call me any time.'

'Is that a promise?'

I didn't answer. Instead, I walked over to him and stretched out my hand. He grabbed hold of it.

Then Mum came in. Of course she thought we were arm-wrestling. 'Stop that at once, Jamie,' she demanded.

'Stop what?' I asked.

'Jamie's been helping me!' exclaimed Harry.

'Has he? Oh, sorry,' said Mum.

'I should think so,' I replied.

'Aunt Nora says you haven't eaten anything all day, Harry. Are you feeling poorly, love?' asked Mum.

'I was, but I'm better now,' said Harry, springing out of bed. 'And I'm starving.'

'Well, there's some chocolate cake left in the kitchen.'

Harry thumped off to the door. 'See you later, Jamie,' he said.

'See you, Harry,' I replied.

Mum watched us, astonished. 'You've certainly cheered Harry up,' she said. 'You know, Harry does look up to you, Jamie.'

Before, I'd have snapped, 'How can he when he's bigger than me?', but today I just murmured, 'Yeah, I think he might do.'

'Now, I've got to look for your dad's fishing rod,' began Mum.

'Why?'

'Your Aunt Nora said she wants to take up fishing. I can't think why.'

Later, when I told Reema about Aunt Nora, she couldn't stop laughing. We were in the garden. Reema's glass of lemonade was so huge she still hadn't finished it, yet it hadn't gone flat at all.

'It's been an incredible day,' said

Reema. 'I just wish we hadn't used up all the cape's magic.'

I took the cape off my shoulders. The gold stars seemed to shine brighter than ever before. And the seven was so dazzling you practically needed sunglasses to look at it.

Was the cape trying to send me a secret message? I think it was.

'Reema,' I said excitedly. 'I'm sure there's still magic in this cape.'

'Are you?' asked Reema eagerly.

'Yeah, lots and lots of it.'

Reema looked as if her birthday had come early. 'Perhaps it's seven wishes a month,' she said.

'Or a week,' I said.

'Or a day!' she cried.

I grinned at her. 'I think the magic has only just begun.'